CHAPTER 1

It's me – Sophie

The school hover-bus dropped me off at
4.28 on the dot, same as ever. It's never
even a micro-second early or a micro-
second late – always 4.28 exactly. It also
dropped me off outside the wrong
house – *that* never changes either.

I grabbed my bag and ran up to the
door of *our* house.

It's me –Sophie.

3

That's my name – Sophie Nova. The house computer recognized my voice; the doors crackled then slid open.

In Ancient History at school we learned that, a long time ago, people used bits of metal called *keys* to open doors! Fancy having to walk around with bits of metal jangling in your pocket! (People weren't too clever in the old days.)

PAUL SHIPTON

Illustrated by Chris Smedley

OXFORD
UNIVERSITY PRESS

OXFORD
UNIVERSITY PRESS

Great Clarendon Street, Oxford OX2 6DP

Oxford University Press is a department of the University of Oxford.
It furthers the University's objective of excellence in research, scholarship,
and education by publishing worldwide in

Oxford   New York

Auckland   Cape Town   Dar es Salaam   Hong Kong   Karachi
Kuala Lumpur   Madrid   Melbourne   Mexico City   Nairobi
New Delhi   Shanghai   Taipei   Toronto

With offices in

Argentina   Austria   Brazil   Chile   Czech Republic   France   Greece
Guatemala   Hungary   Italy   Japan   Poland   Portugal   Singapore
South Korea   Switzerland   Thailand   Turkey   Ukraine   Vietnam

Oxford is a registered trade mark of Oxford University Press
in the UK and in certain other countries

Text © Paul Shipton 1996

The moral rights of the author have been asserted

Database right Oxford University Press (maker)

First published 1996
This edition 2005

British Library Cataloguing in Publication Data
Data available

ISBN-13: 978-0-19-918411-8
ISBN-10: 0-19-918411-9

5 7 9 10 8 6 4

Available in packs
Stage 14 Pack of 6:
ISBN-13: 978-0-19-918406-4; ISBN-10: 0-19-918406-2
Stage 14 Class Pack:
ISBN-13: 978-0-19-918413-2; ISBN-10: 0-19-918413-5
Guided Reading Cards also available:
ISBN-13: 978-0-19-918415-6; ISBN-10: 0-19-918415-1

Cover artwork by Chris Smedley

Printed in Great Britain by
Ashford Colour Press, Gosport Hants

Everything was quiet inside the house, but that didn't mean the place was empty. I stuck my head round the living room door. Yes, there they were – Mum and Dad were plugged into the Ultra-Reality Machine, as usual.

They had bought the machine six months earlier, and since then they had spent all their time on it.

It works like this: you select a programme, then you put this helmet over your head. The machine does the rest. It's as if it plays a film inside your head, only you're part of the film, so it seems like the real world to you.

Sam (that's my brother) and I weren't allowed on it. But Mum and Dad couldn't get enough of it. They only unhooked themselves from the machine to get a quick snack or a few hours' sleep. We hardly ever saw them.

Mum usually ran the Space Wars programme again and again, but Dad liked to vary programmes. He was scowling hard, and so I guessed he was in Caribbean Pirates.

I shook my head. If only they knew how daft they looked! That's when I heard the usual clanking noise from the kitchen.

It was Petey. He was busy pushing the buttons on the Food Dispenser. I said hello, but there was no answer – Petey's Sound Receptors must be on the blink again. I said it louder and he looked up.

Petey wasn't really a 'he' or a 'she'. Petey was an 'it' – a domestic robot. But as his model number was PT–3000, we named him 'Petey', so that made him a 'he'.

'Good afternoon ...' he said in his flat voice. Then he paused while his memory circuits searched for my name. ' ... Sophie.'

Petey was a really old-fashioned model. Dad had said we'd get a new domestic robot, but that was before he had gone and bought the stupid Ultra-Reality Machine. Now it seemed that we just had to put up with the most out-of-date robot in the area. In a way, I didn't mind – Petey had been around for as long as I could remember.

I grinned. Petey had been programmed to be polite, but he only knew a few phrases and they were usually wrong.

But the robot had gone back to his work.

The doors slid open and Sam burst in. He was still wearing his jet-soccer kit, and he didn't look very happy.

My little brother scrunched his face up even more (if that's possible). He gave the jet-pack at his feet a kick.

Sam hated Friday afternoons, because he had to play jet-soccer at school. Some kids flew around with ease, but my brother couldn't get the hang of controlling his jet-pack. To be honest, he was afraid of it.

Dad had said he'd practise with him this summer … But of course that had been before the Ultra-Reality Machine arrived. Now Dad never had time for things like that.

Sam gave a miserable shrug. It was all over – all over until next Friday, that was. He brightened up when his eyes fell on Petey.

What's for dinner, Petey?

The robot buzzed and whirred as it searched for an answer.

'Roast beef, Yorkshire pudding, mashed potatoes and carrots,' he said flatly. He held out a small cup with four pills in it – roast beef, Yorkshire pudding, mashed potatoes and carrots.

Sam gulped them down in one, then gave me a weak smile. All the pills tasted the same, whether you called them roast beef, mashed potatoes or strawberry jelly.

The funny thing is, I thought I saw a smile flash across Petey's face at that moment.

But that was impossible.

Wasn't it?

CHAPTER 2

What's going on?

I had lots of homework that evening.
For history I had to write what a school
day was like in the year 1996. I don't
usually like history, but I liked hearing
what kids did in those days. Do you
know, they used to read from books
and write with little stick-things called
pens. Weird!

Still, I bet it was nice to have a real,
human teacher in the classroom with
you, instead of a Vid-teacher on a
computer screen.

Then for astrophysics I had to design a braking system for the space probe we were building in class. I was right in the middle of a tricky problem, and wishing that Mum could help me (she's a whiz at that sort of stuff). Then Sam poked his head round the door.

That meant it was serious – otherwise little brother would never show his face in my bedroom.

What is it?

Sam shuffled from foot to foot.

It's Petey. He's... well, there's something very odd about him.

I followed Sam. We stopped outside the cupboard where Petey usually recharged himself overnight. The door was closed and some very strange noises were coming from the other side.

And they were getting louder and louder.

Aaaaaaa-aaaaaaa-aaaaaaa-CHOO!

What was going on?

Computer, open the door.

The door slid open and Petey lifted his head. He wasn't plugged in to his recharging socket. But that wasn't the weirdest thing. The weirdest thing was that he was SMILING at us. SMILING!!

Sophie. Sam. Good to see you.

His voice sounded odd too – not the usual flat, machine-like voice. He sounded *sort of* happy to see us.

Er... Petey, what are you doing?

I'm trying to sneeze.

'Trying to sneeze?' echoed Sam in amazement. 'Why?'

Petey scratched his plastic head.

I want to sneeze and I wish to...

Suddenly the robot let out a great rumbling noise: BLAAAAARP!

... and I want to burp, like that. And cough and sniff and yawn and hiccup and feel goose bumps on my arm. And I w-...

Okay, okay, we get the picture. But why?

Again that odd little smile.

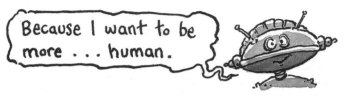

Because I want to be
more . . . human.

I couldn't believe what I was hearing.
This was a *robot* talking – a machine. It
had been designed by someone, then
made in a factory. It had been delivered
to our house in a cardboard box! How
could it be talking like this?

I didn't know what to say. My little
brother looked as stunned as I felt. Then
at last a grin appeared on Sam's face.

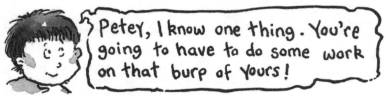

Petey, I know one thing. You're
going to have to do some work
on that burp of yours!

(He should know – I had often
thought that he must be some kind of
world champion at burping.)

But, Petey, being able to sneeze and cough and things like that won't make you more human, you know.

The robot nodded gravely – he knew that.

That is just one of the ways.

I have also begun to write poetry.

Once again my poor old ears couldn't believe what they were hearing.

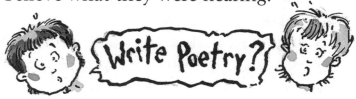

Write Poetry?

'Stop repeating everything he says!' I snapped. 'You sound like a robo-parrot!'

Petey let out a little noise which meant he was clearing his throat (I think).

Here is my first ever poem:

There was a young robot named Neil
That liked to eat things made of steel.
Dessert was tin foil
Which he washed down with oil.
Then he said, 'What a fabulous meal!'

Petey looked at us with hope in his artificial eyes.

What do you think?

It was hard work keeping the smile fixed on my face.

'Not bad,' I lied.

'For a first try,' added Sam.

But my brain was working overtime – how could this be happening? There had to be a reason.

Petey, do you mind if I open up your front panel and take a look inside?

Of course he didn't mind. I whipped my trusty electro-screwdriver from my back pocket and opened the panel at the front of his chest.

Sam and I peered in at the jumble of frayed wires in there.

Bit of a mess isn't it?

Must be ages since anyone looked in here.

I poked around a bit further.

Hold on - what's this?

I pulled out a thick knot of wires to look at it more closely. But then I saw it was more than just wires. There was something in the middle of it – something alive!

It was a tiny brown creature with a little pink nose and a long tail. It let out a tiny squeak.

'What is it?' I yelped.

This was incredible! For the second time that day, Sam's mouth was wide open in amazement.

I think that's called a MOUSE. We did them once at school.

'Wow!' I gasped. 'I've never seen a REAL animal before!' The only animals I had seen were computer simulations in the Virtual Zoo. Oh, and when I was little we had a robo-cat.

But this was different! A real, living animal had made its nest inside Petey. And somehow it had made the robot behave quite differently.

I gently pushed the nest and the little creature back in place.

How does it eat?

It must come out and get stuff from the kitchen, I suppose.

I did up the front panel. Petey watched me. He had been following all of this with interest.

We both looked over to the living room doors. We could hear the low hum of the Ultra-Reality Machine, and I felt as if I could hear the workings of Sam's brain just as clearly.

Next morning...
Tell me the truth - what do you think?
It's very, erm ... life-li

CHAPTER 3

'There's something wrong with him'

The following day we were up good and early – early for us, at any rate.

Petey was ready and waiting for us. Usually at night he went into stand-by mode and recharged his batteries. Not this time – he had spent the whole night working hard.

First he showed us a painting he had made.

Then he asked us to help while he tried on a few new clothes. He wanted a change from his usual uniform. We raided Dad's wardrobe and picked out all the good clothes that Dad never wore any more because they would no longer fit over his belly.

I must admit, Petey looked a bit daft showing off in front of the mirror, but I made sure he didn't see me laugh. After all, I didn't want to hurt his feelings. (Of course, that meant that he *had* feelings to be hurt – and it was becoming pretty clear to me that he *did*.)

That's how the day passed – Petey kept trying out things that he thought 'humans' did.

He even had a go at telling a joke:

Why did the robot cross the road?

I don't know. Why DID the robot cross the road?

Because his On-Board Navigation Unit directed him to.

Sam scratched his chin.

We'll do more work on jokes, I think.

Petey also began to ask us questions, because he said that humans were always curious about the world. (Not Mum and Dad, I thought to myself. Not any more.)

Okay, so his jokes weren't very good, and his questions were a bit strange. But he was trying so hard to get things right, that it was impossible not to like Petey.

He blinked one eye at us several times. I think he was trying to wink.

He said, 'I'm going to make you two some food – *real* food, I mean, like they used to eat in the old days. In my memory files I've found something called a "jam sandwich". I can fiddle with the Food Dispenser so that it will copy the things that go into it.'

Then he smiled and bustled off towards the kitchen.

While he was gone, Sam and I talked about what we should do.

We've got to tell someone. This is too important to keep secret!

But I like him like this! He's much more fun than he used to be! Can't we just wait a few more days? Then we'll tell someone, I promise.

Sam tried to open his eyes as wide as possible and look all innocent – as if a cheap trick like that would make me give in! Well, I *did* give in, but not because of Sam's big, brown eyes. The truth was, I liked playing with Petey too.

Then Mum glided into the room. Her face was pale and dazed-looking. That's how she and Dad always looked when they came off the machine – as if they weren't quite sure where they were.

Hello, darlings. I've just been in the kitchen to get a spot of lunch. Have you noticed how strangely Peter is behaving?

We both said 'No,' like expert liars.

But Mum just shook her head
dreamily.

'No, there's definitely something
wrong with him,' she said. 'I even heard
him singing to himself! But don't worry,
darlings. I called the factory on the vid-
phone. They've sent out a Corrections
Squad van to fix him.'

And with that she drifted back to the
living room where the Ultra-Reality
Machine waited.

CHAPTER 4

Escape!

Fix him!

We raced into the kitchen, where Petey was finishing the ... what had he called them? ... *sandwiches*.

'A Corrections Squad is on its way,' I said. 'They're going to fix you!'

A look of panic appeared on Petey's plastic face. He understood that 'being fixed' meant being turned back into his old self – just a machine.

And that's when I began to wonder. Just how much had Petey really changed?

That meant that the van was racing toward us RIGHT NOW.

But... but... what can we do? We can't out-run a Corrections Squad jet-van.

He looked terrified. He would do anything to get away from the Corrections Squad.

'Yes we can,' said a voice from the doorway. It was Sam.

He had strapped his jet-soccer jet-pack onto his back. In his hands he held out two of Dad's old jet-packs.

We can get away if we use these!

He was grinning, but I knew him too well. I could see the fear in his eyes.

Sam, are you sure?

Sam knew what I meant. He was bad enough with a jet-pack in the jet-soccer playing zone. Flying through the crowded airways of the city was even more difficult ... and dangerous.

But Sam gave a determined nod.

Just then the door buzzer sounded and the house computer announced, 'Visitors!' I took no notice.

Petey and I strapped our jet-packs on.
Then we all hurried out of the back
door. We clicked the packs on, and …

… we zoomed up into the skies.

There was a lot of traffic out for a Saturday afternoon – old couples on slow pleasure rides in their old-fashioned jet-cars; big air-buses full of passengers; teenagers zipping around and looping the loop on flying skateboards.

It was a tough job for the three of us to stick together and not get hit. The question was – which way?

We glanced back and saw a grim sight. The Corrections Squad van was following us.

This Way!

We banked left and whizzed between two tower blocks. Then on toward the city centre.

After a minute or two, we dropped down to the lowest flying level. Now where?

Just then a gruff voice cried out: 'Oy, you three. Stop right there!'

It was a robot traffic controller. We knew we couldn't stop. We zoomed past the robot, leaving it spinning.

I glanced behind again – I could still
see the Corrections Squad van, but it
was further away now. We were going
to make it! We swooped right past the
solar power station.

And that's when things started to go
wrong. My jet-pack began to make a
strange gurgling sound, like water going
down the drain.

It could only mean one thing. The
pack was out of fuel.

CHAPTER 5

Our friend Petey

Well, that's it, I thought glumly – *bye, bye, Petey.*

But Sam let out a shout. I followed his pointing finger.

'We can hide behind that,' he gasped.

The thing he was pointing to was a giant advert which floated over the city.

We flew over to the ad and landed behind it. It was a good thing too – my jet-pack had just about had it.

We peeked out. The repair van was in sight again, but it had slowed right down. They must be wondering which way to go. It looked to me like some terrible flying monster, instead of a van full of repair workers. It edged forward as if it was sniffing the air for our trail.

Close by, Petey looked on in fear. I held my breath. The van began to head off in the opposite direction. But then suddenly it turned.

It was coming our way. It was sure to find us. There was nothing we could do.

At that moment Sam clicked on his jet-pack. He sped out into the skies before us. He dodged skilfully out of the way of an on-coming car, and flew up towards the Corrections Squad van.

He was controlling the jet-pack perfectly. When it really mattered, Sam had forgotten his fear. I felt quite proud of him (though, of course, I would never have told the little squirt that to his face).

Sam hovered in mid-air and began to wave his arms. It wasn't long before the Corrections Squad saw him and started gliding towards him.

'What's he's going to do?' whispered Petey.

I shrugged. 'I suppose he'll tell them that you went the other way. He'll send them off on a wild robo-goose chase. Just sit tight, Petey. We'll make sure you're safe.'

We looked on in silence. The van was not far from Sam now.

But suddenly a dark shape loomed up behind my little brother. It was an air-bus – a big one – and it was heading straight for him.

Sam was watching the Corrections Squad van and he hadn't noticed a thing.

The bus didn't slow down. The robo-driver hadn't spotted Sam. I tried to shout out, but the wind just carried my voice away. I tried to click my jet-pack into life, but it was dead. There was nothing I could do.

I looked at Petey in desperation. He still looked scared ... but suddenly I knew that he was no longer afraid for himself. He was worried *about Sam.*

And there was something else on Petey's face – a new look of determination. That's when I knew he was more than a machine. Far more. He was our *friend*.

And then he was gone.

He blazed up into the air, straight toward Sam. I could see that the Corrections Squad van had spotted him. I'm sure Petey had noticed it too, but he didn't hesitate.

Petey zoomed towards Sam. He shoved him out of the way of the airbus with about two micro-seconds to spare. When Sam saw what had almost happened, his eyes went wide and I saw him hug Petey.

And then the two of them just waited until the Corrections Squad van came to pick them up.

I sat back and did the same.

Fifteen minutes later we were all in the van. Petey sat in the corner with his head hung down.

This was about the fiftieth time the repair robot had said this. I knew it was only following its programming, but it was beginning to get on my nerves.

I leaned forward and tried to sound as menacing as I could.

I didn't go into the details of the 'big trouble'. Luckily, I didn't have to. After a few moments to process the information, the repair robot agreed to take us home.

CHAPTER 6

The beginning of the end

Mum and Dad were hooked up to the Ultra-Reality Machine when we got back. They both looked dazed when they came off it. They blinked as if they had just stepped from darkness into bright light.

Mum shook her head, as if she was shaking away a fog within it.

Sam sighed. I explained once again what had happened.

But... Petey may ACT like a person, but it isn't really one — it's just a machine.

I didn't like the way Mum called Petey 'it'.

The repair robot piped up: 'A machine that needs fixing.'

Dad had a look of sympathy in his glazed eyes.

All those things you told us about... they don't really make Petey human, now do they?

All at once a feeling of anger
swept through me.

I burst out, 'Maybe they don't, but I
know something that does. He went
and saved Sam, even though he *knew*
he'd be caught. Ask him – ask him why
he did it.'

My parents turned toward Petey for
the first time.

'Well?' asked Mum. 'Why?'

Petey slowly looked up.

'Sam's my friend,' repeated the robot. The sincerity in his voice was clear for all to hear.

See! That's more than just human, that's heroic!

Dad gave Mum a puzzled look, and she gave him a puzzled look right back. Petey raised his head hopefully.

I went on, 'And besides ... how can you two talk about behaving like humans? You spend all your time plugged into that stupid machine. Petey knows more about Sam and me than you two. He spends far more time with us!'

Sam grinned and nodded.

For several moments no one moved.

Then slowly Dad stood up, and walked across the room. He pulled the Ultra-Reality Machine plug out of the wall.

I think I've had enough of this for a while.

Me too.

Dad turned to the repair robot.

We won't need any more services today, thanks.

The repair robot grumbled and clanked out of the room. Mum clapped her hands together.

Well, then... Why don't we all go and get a synthi-ice cream? What do you say, Sophie — you, Sam... and Petey.

For the first time in months, I began to see the Mum and Dad I used to know.

And that's when I knew everything was going to be all right.

Some years later

So that's the story of Petey. It all happened a long time ago, but I still remember it well. It's hardly surprising, because NOTHING was the same from that time on.

You see, Petey had started behaving like a human by accident. But it didn't take scientists long to build robots that way on purpose. That meant that we could no longer make robots work like slaves for us. After all, they were thinking creatures now – they had rights too.

A few years later, Petey left our house. He wanted to travel to the outer planets, places robots work and explore where humans could never go.

He's been travelling ever since. He sends me an electronic postcard every so often. The last one said:

And do you know what? I wish I was there too.

Sophie Nova

P.S. Oh, one last thing. The mouse that nested in Petey's chest was taken to the city park. It was a star attraction, and lived out its days in luxury!

About the author

When I was growing up in Manchester, I always wanted to be an astronaut, a footballer, or (if those didn't work out for any reason) perhaps a rock star. So it came as something of a shock when I became first a teacher and then an editor of educational books.

I have lived in Cambridge, Aylesbury, Oxford and Istanbul. I'm still on the run and now live in Chicago with my wife and family.